The Goldfish of Brandy

As told by Stinky the cat

Written and Illustrated by Shannon Rowan

Paperback edition first published in the USA in 2019 by Shannon Rowan

ISBN: 978-1-08-869342-1

For Stinky

"Meow!" (That means 'hello' in *Cat* language, although it can also have many other meanings, as you will learn from my story.)

I am a big silky-haired, black cat and I live in a place called Brandywine Farms. There are no actual farms, but instead it is a place where humans live in houses set upon little hills backed by yards covered in green grass, and filled with birds and butterflies.

I live with a nice family in one of the houses at the end of a short lane. They call me 'Stinky,' but I'm not sure why. I know I don't stink because I groom myself daily. And I used to have a different, longer name which everyone tired of saying, but I can't remember it now.

I have a story to tell you and you may not believe it but I swear that it's true. Here's what happened....

ATTACK
CAT

One rainy afternoon in early spring, the father of the family sat staring at his back garden through the raindrops on the windowpane.

Suddenly, he lifted me to the window and while squeezing me to his chest, he pointed to an extra large drippy raindrop saying, "Do you see that place there? That is where I will have my pond!"

The very next week I heard the sounds of strange men with a big yellow machine in the backyard. I decided it would be best to stay inside the house until they had gone.

By the next morning the noise had stopped and I scampered up to the back door, meowing to be let out.

I crept stealthily to the place where the machine and strangers had been. It was the same place to where the father had pointed the week before. I was somewhat bewildered to see nothing but a deep dark hole in the ground about five feet wide.

"*Big deal,*" I said to myself, "*a hole!*" and went about my business . . .

. . . chasing butterflies and surveying my territory.

The next few days brought rain, lots and lots of rain. They said it was 'raining cats and dogs.' I quickly went to the window to see if there really were cats and dogs falling from the sky. And if so, I planned to help them. Well, the cats, at least.

But there was only rain. So I went back to napping on my favorite feather down blanket.

After a week of rain, the father was very excited about the hole in the back garden. It had filled with water. It was slowly becoming a pond.

He said the next step was to buy some aquatic plants for the pond, such as, water lilies. This didn't sound very interesting to me. I just wanted someone to dish me out some canned tuna.

Some time later, the water lilies were blooming, the sky was blue and the tulips swayed 'round the pond to the tune of the mild spring breeze. But the man was not content. He thought the pond needed something more. In a moment he knew what that something was and rushed off in his car.

An hour later he was back from the pet shop with a bag of seven goldfish for his pond.

The whole family went out to watch the golden shadows in the dark water, swimming to and fro in their new pond home. I watched as well as I sat at the pond's edge, staring for hours, mezmerized.

There was talk of keeping me indoors. They were afraid I was too interested in the fish and that I would try to eat them. What they didn't know was that I wasn't interested in catching the fish. I hate getting my paws wet! Ick! I was actually communicating with the fish family. (It just looked like staring, to the humans.)

For it was in fact a family- a mama and papa fish plus their five baby fish. The goldfish liked their new home. They said it was much better than living in an aquarium. So they told me all about it.

As the hot days of summer wore on, I often visited the goldfish family, sitting by the water, under the shade of a small nearby cherry tree.

Each time I visited I noticed something remarkable.

The family was rapidly multiplying and every time I sat at the water's edge, there shone a new golden light from within. Until finally, all I could see was one big mass of orange.

The mother fish complained to me of their crowded situation . . .

"Oh, it's just too much, Mr. Stinky. I can't bear it anymore! I can't sleep for all of the movement and bubbly sounds. And then the young ones start to fight and nip each other and they sometimes even bite ME– their own mother! And I don't mind being close to them but to swim through nothing but slimy bodies all day is just too much!"

I tried to console her by telling her that I would come up with a plan to unburden her. But I really didn't know what I, a mere cat, could do for her.

It wasn't too long before the man and his family noticed the teeming conditions in their pond. There was even talk of using the bathtubs to house the extra fish. But the girls wouldn't have it.

"How am I to take a bath with those slimy creatures in there! No way!" they cried.

A few days later, the rain returned. There were fierce thunderstorms and a hurricane watch in effect. We were all forced to stay indoors for the time being. I watched the pond from my perch on the windowsill.

To my amazement, I saw little orange shapes jumping up into the air from the pond's waters. They landed in puddles that had formed nearby. It worried me to see the fish scattered over the lawn in this way.

From another windowsill I noticed that a small stream had formed alongside the house, down the hill of the driveway into the road, filling the streets wtih water.

I was struck with a great idea. But it meant doing something I hated more than anything in the world- getting wet!

Yet I had to risk it in order to save the goldfish family.

I began to meow loudly by the front door. The aunt of the family appeared and said,

"But Stinky, you don't want to go out, it's raining! You'll get wet!"

"Meow, meow, meow, meow, MEOW!" I cried desperately.

Finally she consented.

"Okay, if you insist. But, you'll be sorry!"

The door opened and I ran quickly to the pond. I shouted my plans to the mother fish over the noise of the storm, while ducking under the cherry tree, trying to keep the rain off of my fur.

The mother agreed and wished me luck. She then told all of her children my plan. With a few brief farewells, the fish and I were off and on our way.

They hopped along behind me from puddle to puddle and then into the newly formed stream. Down they went, gliding through the wet grass on the hill down to the road.

On the pavement they swam in the waters of the flooded street. I walked along side them leading the way, in the marshy grasses of the neighbors' lawns, through the horrible wet, wet rain.

We traveled a couple of miles this way, at times being nearly missed by passing cars that drenched my precious fur with their spray.

A few hours, nearly one hundred exhausted fish and a sopping wet cat later, we had arrived at our destination- the Loch Raven reservoir.

Mustering up all the remaining energy they had left, the fish leaped one by one into the massive reservoir. Near the end, a couple of the smaller fish needed extra help. So I carefully picked them up with my paws and released them into the great body of water.

I have to admit that I was momentarily tempted to have a tasty goldfish snack as they flopped about on my paws. But I remembered my promise to the mother fish and let them go.

I was wet and weary, but happy to see a golden glimmer of goodbyes coming from the reservoir as I turned to go home.

Once home I was lovingly taken indoors, dried off and placed on a warm quilt.

The family had been worried, but also scolded me in case I had eaten the fish, which had so mysteriously and quickly disappeared from their pond.

I tried to explain, "meow, meow, meow, MEOW!"

But no one listened.

Later on, I told the mother goldfish of her children's safe journey and arrival at the reservoir.

She thanked me and vowed to not have anymore baby fish thereafter. It would mean an early retirement for the mamma and pappa fish, something for which they were more than ready.

From that day on, I heard it told that as you drive over the Loch Raven reservoir you might notice something new, extra ripples on the surface and a slight change of color in the water; an added touch of gold.

The End

Special thanks to:

My loving partner Sam Janesko for his tireless support and belief in my talents.

. . . the Bishop family for hosting Stinky 6 years of his life, we are both very grateful. With a special thanks to Aunt Lucy for all of her extra care for Stinky, opening the door at his scratching at all hours, changing his litter box, feeding and brushing and loving him.

. . . my best friends and gifted writers for their unending support, encouragement and editing help:

Sara Kelleher
Kathy Cottle

. . . and for additional editing help from my dear friends & family:

Heather Bishop
Christine Turner
Christian Jusinski
Jennifer Kaufmann
Jimmy Bishop
Richard Bishop

And thank you to my other wonderful close friends who've cheered me along the way!

You can find more work by Shannon Rowan here:

www.shannonrowan.com

About the Author/Illustrator

Shannon Rowan

.. rescued "Stinky" at 5 months old at an animal shelter in Utah, but as the saying goes, he really rescued her. He was a loving companion, best friend to Shannon and well loved by many. They spent 20 good years together in Provo Ut, Brooklyn, NY, Fallston, MD, and Washington, DC, before Stinky's passing on Valentine's day, 2014. This book, with its story passed onto Shannon by Stinky, is dedicated to his memory.

Shannon has been drawing pictures since the age of 2 and taking photographs since the age of 12. With a BFA in Design/Photography Shannon has published stories, photography and art in numerous national and international magazines and books. She is also a professional level hula hoop dancer and musician.

This is her first illustrated children's book.

About the story teller

Stinky

A truly unique individual. Very fond of people and especially children. Well into his old age he loved when his family's grandkids came to pet and brush him.

Extremely intellegent for his species, it did seem he was able to communicate with humans and other animals. He did in fact live in a place called Brandywine Farms with the author's family for a number of years. And he did sit for many hours watching the goldfish swim in the pond. As to the rest of the story, we'll have to take him at his word.

Made in the USA
Columbia, SC
13 March 2020